D1442369

Wind River

Stories™

COYOTE
& the Rock

A story by Rupert Weeks
Illustrated by Jon Cox

Other **Wind River Stories**™ titles:

Crazy Man & the Plums
Fox & the Woodtick
Yuse, the Bully & the Bear
Yuse & the Spirit

Published by Painted Pony, Inc.
Copyright 2005 - Painted Pony, Inc.
All rights reserved
Printed by Global Interprint, Inc.
First Edition

ISBN - 0-9759806-2-9
Library of Congress Control Number: 2005905285

Special thanks to:
The Rupert Weeks Family
John Washakie
Scott Ratliff
Quinn Carroll
The Wyoming Department of Education
The Wind River Development Fund

Story used with permission of Mildred D. Weeks
Edited by Linda Stoval
Word translations by Mildred D. Weeks
Caption translations by Mildred D. Weeks and C. S.

P.O. Box 661
Ft. Washakie, WY 82514
www.paintedponyinc.com

Printed in Hong Kong

Forward

The story, "Coyote & the Rock," is an amusing tale that teaches us the value of honesty. Reading about Coyote's misadventure and bad behavior, children are reminded that bad choices have negative consequences. Wise teachers, like Fox in this story, are here to guide us and help us make good decisions. But ultimately, we each must make our own choices and live with their outcomes.

Coyote & the Rock is one book in a series that celebrate the culture and stories of Wyoming's American Indian Heritage. These books are presented to Wyoming's children not only as a gift from the Wyoming Department of Education, but as a vital part of our state's history and culture to be discovered and shared.

Through this project, the Wyoming Department of Education shows its pride and commitment to all of Wyoming's people. These wonderful stories have become reality because of the collaborative work between many partners: the Arapaho and Shoshone tribes, Wyoming educators, American Indian authors, illustrators, the publishers and the Wyoming Department of Education.

We hope that you will enjoy and share this book, now and for years to come.

Wyoming Department of Education

Dedication

The story of Coyote & the Rock is dedicated to Mr. Weeks. He loved telling stories and talking about the history of the Wind River Reservation and Shoshone culture to his students, both Indian and non-Indian.

While he was working on his class lessons, sometimes we would hear his chuckle and know he was working on his Coyote story for the next day.

The Weeks Family

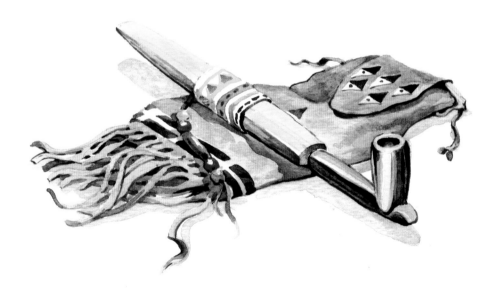

One day Fox was walking in the woods. He was humming a happy song. He had a new necklace made of pretty beads.

Wah-nea Zand Na-vund Zoe-oh Go-dook-ge-gaunt.

All the other animals liked his necklace. His friends asked to look at his necklace more closely. "Good morning, Fox," said Deer. "What a pretty necklace you have!"

"T hank you," smiled Fox.

"Good morning, Fox," said Porcupine. "May I feel the beads of your necklace?"

"No," said Fox. "One of your quills might poke me, but you can look."

Porcupine moved closer and looked at the beads. "Oh, they are very fine beads."

Coyote was coming down the path. He saw all the animals around Fox and pushed to the front.

"What is going on here?" Coyote asked.

"Fox has a very pretty necklace," said Beaver, "and we are all looking at it."

"Move and let me look, too," Coyote snapped.

E-zah-pah Wa-sup-ped Ma-nah-gwath Vuook.

Then he grabbed the necklace and tried to pull it from Fox's neck! The necklace would not come off.

Fox looked at Coyote.

"You don't have to take my beads. You can get some beads of your own," he said. "Go to Rock and ask for beads. But you must pay for the beads or you will be sorry!"

E-zah-pah Wan-nea Go-dook Za-du-natch Ma-voogh.

"I will pay Rock for the beads," Coyote said with a smile. "I always pay a fair price. I would never cheat anyone."

The other animals knew that was not true. Coyote had tricked many of them in the past, but they did not say anything to him. Coyote trotted away to visit Rock.

W hen Coyote saw Rock he smiled and acted like a friend.

"Hello, Rock," said Coyote, "I have always liked you, because you are a very nice rock."

Coyote smiled so big that it made his teeth shine in the sun.

Coyote waited for Rock to answer, but Rock sat still and said nothing.

Coyote got angry and said, "Give me some beads, Rock!"

Rock gave Coyote some very pretty beads. The greedy Coyote grinned and thought, 'This Rock can't do anything to me. I will run away without paying!' And he ran as fast as he could go.

A few days later, greedy Coyote wanted more beads.

"I will trick Rock again," he said to himself. He went back to Rock and said, "Give me some beads and I will pay you well."

Rock gave him more beautiful beads. Coyote was very excited. He looked at Rock and thought, 'He can't do anything if I run away.' So, he ran away without paying again.

E-zah-pah E-ge-daugh Dim-be Zoe-oh Yeh-quos Due-na-chew.

As Coyote ran along the path, he met Fox. Fox saw Coyote's beads and said, "I hope you paid Rock for the beads, Coyote."

Coyote lied, "Of course I paid him! I would never cheat Rock."

"That's good," said Fox, "because if you cheat Rock, you will be very sorry."

Coyote's face looked very serious, but inside he was laughing. 'Fox is dumb,' he thought, 'he pays for beads from Rock when he could just take them.' He laughed and laughed to himself about Fox.

Dim-be Ah-quin-tant E-zah-pah Vayth.

Later that day, Coyote came to the river and sat down. He had rested for some time when he heard a strange sound behind him. He looked back and saw Rock far behind him on the path.

'I am not scared,' he thought. 'Rock rolls very slowly. I can run much faster and get away.'

Still, Coyote decided to move, just in case. He tiptoed along the riverbank very quietly, then stopped and looked back.

Rock was still there, rolling closer to him. Coyote said, "That Rock could never catch me." But he was a little scared, so he walked faster.

Coyote heard Rock going faster, too.

'Rock can only roll
down a hill,' thought Coyote, 'I can run anywhere.'

He followed a path up a hill, sure that he was safe there.

In a few minutes, Coyote heard Rock behind him, rolling faster than before. He ran through a very small space between two walls of rock. 'Now I am safe,' Coyote thought.

But Rock, going very fast, broke right through the rock walls!

"Help me! Help me!" Coyote yelled as he ran even faster on the path.

He passed Bear who was digging for wild carrots.

E-zah-pah Ah-qui De-vaint Neh De-wa-za-woin.

"What is it, Coyote?" asked Bear as Coyote ran by him.

"Bear," cried Coyote, "Rock is trying to kill me! Get on the path behind me. Rock will stop for you!"

Bear got on the path and saw Rock coming very fast.

"Stop!" yelled Bear. But Rock rolled right over Bear and kept going.

C oyote was very scared now.

He saw Elk and cried, "Help! Rock is trying to kill me! Get behind me! Rock will stop for you!"

E

lk got behind him and turned his big antlers toward Rock.

"Good day, Friend," he said to Rock.

Rock rolled right over him and left him flat. Coyote looked back and was very, very scared.

oon Coyote came to Fox who was hunting for food.

"Fox, my friend! Rock is trying to kill me. Make him stop!"

"Did you pay for your beads, Coyote?" Fox asked.

"No," Coyote answered.

"Then I can not help you," Fox said.

Wah-nea E-zah-pah Ni-quick Na-Gay De-wa-zoi-wyat.

Fox looked and saw Rock following Coyote going very fast. Coyote was tired and was not running so fast now. Rock rolled right behind Coyote, then rolled on top of him and stopped! Only Coyote's tail was sticking out.

Other animals came and saw Rock on top of Coyote.

Wa-sup-peney O-vuook Dim-be E-zah-pah Vah Gaw-t-ook.

"What happened? Why did Rock roll over Coyote?" they asked.

Fox answered, "Because Coyote cheated Rock and did not pay for what he got."

And that is the end of Coyote...

...for now!

Illustration Captions

Page 6. *Wah-nea Zand Na-vund Zoe-oh Go-dook-ge-gaunt.*
Fox had a necklace made of pretty beads.

Page 12. *E-zah-pah Wa-sup-ped Ma-nah-gwath Vuook.*
Coyote saw the other animals in the distance.

Page 13. *E-zah-pah Wan-nea Go-dook Za-du-natch Ma-voogh.*
Coyote tried to pull the necklace from Fox's neck!

Page 17. *E-zah-pah E-ge-daugh Dim-be Zoe-oh Yeh-quos Due-na-chew.*
Coyote ran away with Rock's beads again.

Page 19. *Dim-be Ah-quin-tant E-zah-pah Vayth.*
Rock was rolling towards Coyote.

Page 23. *E-zah-pah Ah-qui De-vaint Neh De-wa-za-woin.*
Coyote asks Bear to help him.

Page 27. *Wah-nea E-zah-pah Ni-quick Na-Gay De-wa-zoi-wyat.*
Fox told Coyote he could not help him.

Page 28. *Wa-sup-peney O-vuook Dim-be E-zah-pah Vah Gaw-t-ook.*
The animals saw Rock on top of Coyote.

Glossary

Shoshone word	English word
1. E-zah-pah	Coyote
2. Wah-nea	Fox
3. Dim-be	Rock
4. So-go-dee-he-ah	Elk
5. Be-ya-gway-ish or Haw-nee	Beaver
6. Ah-qui	Bear
7. Yuh-a-zee	Porcupine
8. Zoe-oh	Beads
9. Wee-you	Needle
10. Did-dah-hoe-dah	Digging
11. Ee-shaw-vake	Trick
12. Gway-ish	Tail
13. Yump	Wild Carrots
14. Dee-yah-soy	Afraid/Scared
15. Hy-inge	Friend

1918 - 1983

"ONLY THOSE BORN IN THE HOT SUMMER MONTHS ARE ABLE TO TELL COYOTE STORIES." - Rupert Weeks

Rupert Weeks was born July 24, 1918 in Garland, Utah to Nesbitt and Sylvia (Tyboats) Weeks. His family later moved to Fort Hall, Idaho where Mr. Weeks attended the Fort Hall Indian boarding school. When he was 16, his family moved to Fort Washakie, on the Wind River Indian Reservation in Central Wyoming. There he attended the Fort Washakie Indian Boarding School.

Mr. Weeks served in the United States Army from 1943-1945, where he fought in the Battle of the Bulge.

After returning from the war, he was actively involved in his community. Mr. Weeks served on the Shoshone Entertainment Committee, Shoshone Oil and Gas Commission, and was on the first Wyoming Indian High School Board of Directors. He also was an interpreter for Shoshone Tribal meetings and acted as a consultant and teacher for native studies programs.

The Shoshone cultural center built in Fort Washakie in 2003 was named the Rupert Weeks Traditional Center in Mr. Weeks' memory.

His wife Mildred and children Ivan, Kassel, Gary, Samuel, Nola, Betty, Connie and his stepson Phillip Hurtado reside on the Wind River Indian Reservation in Wyoming.

His parents, his brother Edgar and his children Violet and Rupert Jr. preceded Mr. Weeks in death.

Jon T. Cox

"I grew up in Cheyenne, Wyoming and graduated from East High School, The University of Wyoming and most importantly, the school of life. I have had a variety of occupations and been many things in my time. I owe a great deal of these experiences, successes and strengths to my parents, sister, brother and family. My wife, Tammy, and my children, Kelly, Katy and Jon, have allowed me to be whatever I dreamed. I love them all. From the experience of raising and contributing to a family, one learns a lot about life and the lessons it presents for passage through it. Another passion and love of mine is gardening. My wife has taught me a great deal about it and is the real gardener. I am really just the lawn boy.

One of the people who taught me other important life lessons was Professor Victor Flach, who directed my Masters' program. He believed that we must make a record of our experiences. If we do not, then we must ask, did they ever happen? Although only a story, this book is a record and vital part of Native American culture that must not be allowed to disappear. I consider it a privilege to have been allowed to record this traditional story through my illustrations."

Mr. Cox and his wife live in Riverton, Wyoming.